GUESS
HOW MUCH
I LOVE YOU

TENTH
ANNIVERSARY
EDITION

To Liz with love,
A. J.

Text copyright © 1994 by Sam McBratney
Illustrations copyright © 1994 by Anita Jeram

Guess How Much I Love You™ is a registered trademark of
Walker Books Ltd., London.

First U.S. slipcase edition 2005

Library of Congress Cataloging-in-Publication Data

McBratney, Sam.
Guess how much I love you / by Sam McBratney ;
illustrated by Anita Jeram. — 1st U.S. ed.
Summary: During a bedtime game, every time Little Nutbrown Hare
demonstrates how much he loves his father, Big Nutbrown Hare gently
shows him that the love is returned even more.
ISBN 1-56402-473-3 (reinforced trade edition)
ISBN 0-7636-2435-7 (slipcase edition)
ISBN 0-7636-2729-1 (signed slipcase edition)
[1. Hares—Fiction.   2. Fathers and sons—Fiction.   3. Bedtime—
Fiction.   4. Love—Fiction.]   I. Jeram, Anita, ill.   II. Title.
PZ7.M47826Gu   1995
[E]—dc20   94-1599

10 9 8 7 6 5 4 3 2

Printed in Singapore

The illustrations in this book were done in watercolor and ink.

Candlewick Press
2067 Massachusetts Avenue
Cambridge, Massachusetts 02140

visit us at www.candlewick.com

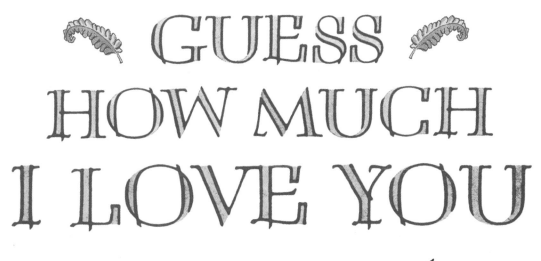

GUESS HOW MUCH I LOVE YOU

by
Sam McBratney

illustrated by
Anita Jeram

CANDLEWICK PRESS
CAMBRIDGE, MASSACHUSETTS

Little Nutbrown Hare,
who was going to bed, held
on tight to Big Nutbrown Hare's
very long ears.

He wanted to be sure that Big
Nutbrown Hare was listening.
"Guess how much
I love you," he said.

"Oh, I don't think I could guess that,"
said Big Nutbrown Hare.

"This much," said Little
Nutbrown Hare, stretching out
his arms as wide as they could go.

Big Nutbrown Hare had even longer arms. "But I love *you* this much," he said.

Hmm, that is a lot, thought Little Nutbrown Hare.

"I love you
as high as
I can reach,"
said Little
Nutbrown
Hare.

"I love you as high as *I* can reach," said Big Nutbrown Hare.

That is very
high, thought
Little Nutbrown
Hare. I wish
I had arms
like that.

Then Little
Nutbrown Hare
had a good idea.
He tumbled
upside down
and reached
up the tree
trunk with
his feet.

"I love you
all the way up
to my toes!"
he said.

"And *I* love you
all the way up
to your toes," said
Big Nutbrown Hare,
swinging him up
over his head.

"I love you
as high as
I can hop!"
laughed Little
Nutbrown Hare,

bouncing up

and down.

"But I love you as high as
I can hop," smiled Big
Nutbrown Hare—and he
hopped so high that his ears
touched the branches above.

That's good
hopping,
thought
Little
Nutbrown
Hare.
I wish I
could hop
like that.

"I love you all the way down the
lane as far as the river," cried
Little Nutbrown Hare.

"I love you across the river
and over the hills," said
Big Nutbrown Hare.

That's very far, thought
Little Nutbrown Hare.

He was almost too sleepy
to think anymore.

Then he looked beyond the
thornbushes, out into the big
dark night. Nothing could
be farther than the sky.

"I love you right up to
the moon," he said,
and closed his eyes.

"Oh, that's far," said
Big Nutbrown Hare.
"That is very,
very far."

Big Nutbrown Hare settled
Little Nutbrown Hare
into his bed of leaves.

He leaned over
and kissed him
good night.

Then he lay down close by
and whispered with a smile,
"I <u>love</u> <u>you</u> <u>right</u> up <u>to</u> the <u>moon</u>—

<u>and</u> <u>back</u>."

I LOVE YOU WHOLE SKY AND BACK AGAIN
AMANDA LYNNE!

Always~Liz

2006

GUESS HOW MUCH I LOVE YOU

TENTH ANNIVERSARY EDITION

Say to someone special . . .

"I love you right up to the moon — and back."

First published a decade ago, this simple yet profound tale is now available in
thirty-seven languages and has sold more than fifteen million copies worldwide.
To celebrate the tenth anniversary of this beloved picture book, Candlewick Press
is pleased to offer this beautiful clothbound, slipcased gift edition.

Includes a FREE CD featuring a special reading of *Guess How Much I Love You.*

A NOTE FROM THE AUTHOR

*"This evening, somewhere in the world a mum or dad will
be reading* Guess How Much I Love You *with a little
one who really matters. The story is simple and natural.
For my own part, the story was written mainly to be fun,
and Anita's lovely drawings are a perfect match for the text.*

*"I'd like to share with you just one thought a father sent
to me. He said, 'On good nights my little boy loves me to
the moon and back, but on bad nights he only loves me to
the door and back.' If you're a parent, here's hoping that
you mostly make it to the moon."*

Sam McBratney

A NOTE FROM THE ILLUSTRATOR

*"I can't believe that it's ten years since the Nutbrown Hares
appeared in our lives. All sorts of things have changed in
the world since then, but they will never grow older and the
sentiment they express will last forever. For me, I'd like
to hold on tight to Big Nutbrown Hare's ears and whisper,
'Thank you.'"*

Anita Jeram

$20.00 U.S.
$28.00 Canada

CANDLEWICK PRESS
www.candlewick.com

ISBN 076362435-7
52000>

9 780763 624354

All Wrapped Up
800-921-7873
Gift Wrap and Gift Bags

The Art Group
978-762-8612
www.artgroup.com
Prints

**Bronner's Christmas
Wonderland**
989-652-9931
www.bronners.com
Ornaments

Candamar Designs
800-854-7161
www.candamar.com
Embroidery Kits

Casa D'Oro
866-333-7873
www.italiangoldcharms.com
Modular Charms

Duni Corporation
800-237-8270
www.duni.com
Party Goods

Fabrics by Spectrix
212-629-8320
Fabric

Galison Books/Mudpuppy Press
212-354-8840
www.mudpuppy.com
Floor Puzzle and Mini Prints

Genius Products
858-793-8840
www.geniusproducts.com
*Audiotapes and CDs featuring
lullabies and classical music*

Kushies Baby Products
905-643-9118
www.kushies.com
Apparel and Accessories

LeapFrog
800-701-LEAP
www.leapfrog.com
Electronic Read-Along Books

Mermaid Theatre of Nova Scotia
902-798-5841
www.mermaidtheatre.ns.ca
Theatrical Show with Puppets

MM's Designs
713-461-2600
www.mmsdesigns.com
Stationery and Wooden Room Décor

Peaceable Kingdom Press
800-444-7778
www.pkpress.com
*Greeting Cards, Notecard
Portfolios, Bookmarks, and
Calendars*

Salamander Graphix
800-451-5311
www.salamandergraphix.com
Night-Lights, Totes, and Umbrellas

Scene Weaver
803-252-0662
www.sceneweaver.com
Tapestry Throws and Pillows

Stephan Enterprises
800-359-2917
www.stephanenterprises.com
*Water-Filled Place Mats,
Melamine Feeding Sets, First Curl
Container, and Helpful Hare*

Sunshine n' Kisses
877-615-2229
www.babyuniverse.com
Bedding and Bedding Accessories

Wallables
310-416-9999
www.wallables.com
Shaped Soft Wall Décor

Wildkin
303-652-9130
www.wildkin.com
*Plush Backpacks, Plush Purse
Pals, and Wooden Height Charts*

Wink, Inc.
303-546-0008
www.winkinc-link.com
*Wooden Room Accessories and
Wooden Toys*

York Wallcoverings
717-846-4456
www.yorkwall.com
Borders and Wall Coverings